17

My First Time

Starting School

Kate Petty, Lisa Kopper, and Jim Pipe

Stargazer Books

© Aladdin Books Ltd 2008

Designed and produced by
Aladdin Books Ltd

First published in 2008
in the United States by
Stargazer Books
c/o The Creative Company
123 South Broad Street
Mankato, Minnesota 56002

Printed in the United States
All rights reserved

Illustrator: Lisa Kopper

Photocredits:
All photos from istockphoto.com except 5—Brand X.

Library of Congress Cataloging-in-Publication Data

Petty, Kate.
  Starting school / by Kate Petty.
     p. cm. -- (My first time)
  Includes Index.
   ISBN 978-1-59604-155-4 (alk. paper)
   [1. Schools--Fiction.] I. Title.
PZ7.P44814St 2007
[Fic]--dc22
                    2007001766

About this book

New experiences can be scary for young children. This series will help them to understand situations they may find themselves in, by explaining in a friendly way what can happen.

This book can be used as a starting point for discussing issues. The questions in some of the boxes ask children about their own experiences.

The stories will also help children to master basic reading skills and learn new vocabulary.

It can help if you read the first sentence to children, and then encourage them to read the rest of the page or story. At the end, try looking through the book again to find where the words in the glossary are used.

Contents

Today is Sam's first day at school.
Mom and Jenny are taking him there.

Dad says goodbye at the end of the road.
"Be good, Sam, and have a nice day."

Sam sees lots of children on the way. They wave and shout to each other.

He wonders who else is starting school for the very first time today.

Some children take the bus to school.

5

Sam's new teacher is there to meet him.

"Hello, Sam. I'm Miss Smith.
Here's your peg. It has your name on
it with a picture of a pig underneath."

6

"Maria is new today too.
Why don't you both come along with me?"

Sam just wants to hold Mom's hand.
He feels a little strange and shy.

Some children are putting on their aprons.
They are going to do some painting.

"Would you like to paint something too?"
Sam pulls an apron over his head.

Sam is ready to start painting so Mom says she'll leave him now.

But Jenny doesn't want to go! Sam says he'll paint a picture just for her.

What do you like to draw or paint?

Sam enjoys painting his picture.

He doesn't really notice when Mom and Jenny go to do some shopping. They won't be gone for long.

Sam sees that Maria is crying.
He goes to find out why.

Someone has knocked over her tower of blocks.
Sam helps her build it up again.

It's time to play outside in the sun.
One at a time on the slide!

Sam wants to go in the pedal car
but the teacher tells him to wait.

12

"You must take turns," says the teacher.
"Will you let Maria go first?"

Maria has a turn, then a bell starts to ring.
They have to go back inside.

Sam wants to know where the bathrooms are.
Miss Smith shows him the way.

He washes and dries his hands.
Now he's ready for a drink.

14

Maria has already
finished her drink.
Sam is thirsty. He drinks very fast.

He wants to go outside again
to have his turn in the car.

A glass of milk
is good for you.

15

"The car must wait until tomorrow, Sam.
We've got some work to do now."

"I want you to find another shape
like this one. Can you do it?"

Sam hopes that he can.
"There it is. This is fun.
What else should I find?"

"Try the square and
the circle next."

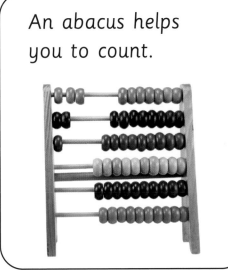

An abacus helps
you to count.

17

Miss Smith will read them a story now,
so they must all stop talking.

Sam turns to Maria but she says, "Sssh!"
So he settles down to listen quietly.

The story is about a spider.
They sing about a spider too.

The children know some
actions for the song.
Sam finds he can soon join in.

Can you clap
and sing?

19

It's time to go home already.
Mom and Jenny are waiting for Sam.

"Where's your coat, Sam? Find your peg."
"Here it is—it's the one with the pig."

20

Sam sings his spider song all the way home.
He's looking forward to school tomorrow.

He'll have his ride in the pedal car
and see Maria—his new friend.

teacher

pegs

painting

blocks

play

working

story time

singing

23

Index

Find out more

Find out about your child's first day at school at:

http://www.pbs.org/parents/goingtoschool/before_school.html
http://www.pitara.com/parenting/school/preschool.asp
http://www.usa.gov/topics/Back_to_School.shtml
http://cbs2.com/local/local_story_215210922.html